Dick King-Smith served in the Grenadier Guards during the Second World War, and afterwards spent twenty years as a farmer in Gloucestershire, the county of his birth. Many of his stories are inspired by his farming experiences. Later he taught at a village primary school. His first book, *The Fox Busters*, was published in 1978. Since then he has written a great number of children's books, including *The Sheep-Pig* (winner of the Guardian Award and filmed as *Babe*), *Harry's Mad*, *Noah's Brother*, *The Hodgeheg*, *Martin's Mice*, *Ace*, *The Cuckoo Child* and *Harriet's Hare* (winner of the Children's Book Award in 1995). At the British Book Awards in 1991 he was voted Children's Author of the Year. He has three children, a large number of grandchildren and several great-grandchildren, and lives in a seventeenth-century cottage, only a crow's-flight from the house where he was born.

Dick King-Smith
Blessu

Illustrated by Adrienne Kennaway

PUFFIN BOOKS

PUFFIN BOOKS

Published by the Penguin Group
Penguin Books Ltd, 80 Strand, London WC2R 0RL, England
Penguin Group (USA), Inc., 375 Hudson Street, New York, New York 10014, USA
Penguin Books Australia Ltd, 250 Camberwell Road, Camberwell, Victoria 3124, Australia
Penguin Books Canada Ltd, 10 Alcorn Avenue, Toronto, Ontario, Canada M4V 3B2
Penguin Books India (P) Ltd, 11 Community Centre, Panchsheel Park, New Delhi – 110 017, India
Penguin Books (NZ) Ltd, Cnr Rosedale and Airborne Roads, Albany, Auckland, New Zealand
Penguin Books (South Africa) (Pty) Ltd, 24 Sturdee Avenue, Rosebank 2196, South Africa

Penguin Books Ltd, Registered Offices: 80 Strand, London WC2R 0RL, England

www.penguin.com

First published by Hamish Hamilton Ltd 1990
Published in Puffin Books 1995
Published in this edition 2002
10

Text copyright © Fox Busters Ltd, 1990
Illustrations copyright © Adrienne Kennaway, 1990
All rights reserved

The moral right of the author and illustrator has been asserted

Printed in Singapore by Star Standard

British Library Cataloguing in Publication Data
A CIP catalogue record for this book is available from the British Library

ISBN-13:978-0-14131-293-4

B lessu was a very small elephant
when he sneezed for the first time.

The herd was moving slowly
through the tall elephant-grass,
so tall that it hid the legs of his
mother and his aunties, and reached
halfway up the bodies of his bigger
brothers and sisters.

But you couldn't see Blessu at all.
Down below, where he was
walking, the air was thick with pollen
from the flowering elephant-grasses,
and suddenly Blessu felt a strange
tickly feeling at the base of his very
small trunk.

Shutting his eyes and closing his mouth, he stuck his very small trunk straight out before him, and sneezed:

"AAARCHOOO!"

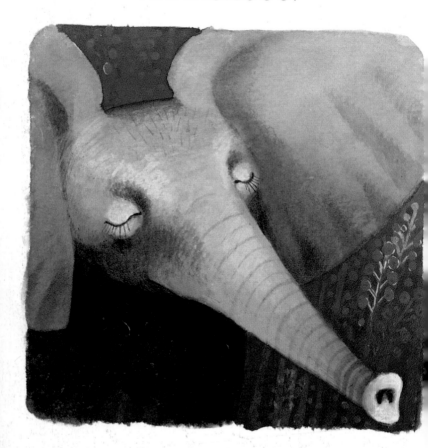

4

It wasn't the biggest sneeze in the world, but it was very big for a very small elephant.

"BLESS YOU!"

cried his mother and his aunties and
his bigger brothers and sisters.

For a moment Blessu looked rather cowed. He did not know what they meant, and he thought he might have done something naughty. He hung his head and his ears drooped.

But the herd moved on through the tall elephant-grass without taking any further notice of him, so he soon forgot to be unhappy.

Before long, Blessu gave another
sneeze, and another, and another,
and each time he sneezed, his
mother and his aunties and his
bigger brothers and sisters cried:

"BLESS YOU!"

They did not say this to any of
the other elephants, Blessu noticed
(because none of the other elephants
sneezed), so he thought, "That must
be my name."

At last the herd came out of the tall elephant-grass and went down to the river, to drink and to bathe, and Blessu stopped sneezing.

"Poor baby!" said his mother, touching the top of his hairy little head gently with the tip of her trunk. "You've got awful hay fever."

"And what a sneeze he's got!"
said one of his aunties. "It's not the
biggest sneeze in the world, but it's
very big for a very small elephant."

The months passed, and Blessu
grew, very slowly, as elephants do.
But so did his hay fever. Worse and
worse it got and more and more he
sneezed as the herd moved through
the tall elephant-grass.

Every few minutes Blessu would
shut his eyes and close his mouth
and stick his very small trunk
straight out before him and sneeze:

"AAAARCHOOOO!!"

And each time he sneezed, his
mother and his aunties and his
bigger brothers and sisters cried:

"BLESS YOU!"

But though Blessu was not growing very fast, one bit of him was.

It was his trunk. All that sneezing was stretching it.

Soon he had to carry it tightly curled up, so as not to trip on it.

"Poor baby!" said his mother. "At this rate your trunk will soon be as long as mine."

But Blessu only answered:

"AAAARCHOOOO!!"

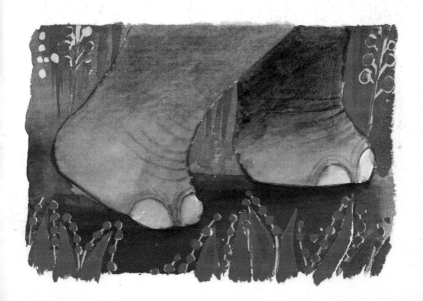

"Don't worry, my dear," said one
of his aunties. "The longer the
better, I should think. He'll be able
to reach higher up into the trees
than any elephant ever has, and
he'll be able to go deeper into the
river (using his trunk as a snorkel)."

"Ah well," said Blessu's mother. "Soon the elephant-grass will finish flowering, and the poor little chap will stop sneezing."

And it did.

And he did.

The years passed, and each year brought the season of the flowering of the elephant-grasses that shed their pollen and made Blessu sneeze.

And each sneeze stretched that trunk of his just a little bit further.

By the time he was five years old, he could reach as high into the trees, and go as deep into the river (using his trunk as a snorkel) as his mother and his aunties.

By the time he was ten years old,
he could reach higher and go deeper.

And by the time Blessu was twenty years old, and had grown a fine pair of tusks, he had, without doubt, the longest trunk of any elephant in the whole of Africa.

And now, in the season of the flowering of the elephant-grasses, what a sneeze he had!

Shutting his eyes, and closing his mouth, he stuck his amazing long trunk straight out before him and sneezed:

"AAAAAARCHOOOOOOO!!!"

Woe betide anything that got in the way of that sneeze!

Young trees were uprooted, birds
were blown whirling into the sky,
small animals like antelope and
gazelle were bowled over and over,
larger creatures such as zebra and
wildebeest stampeded in panic before
that mighty blast, and even the
King of the Beasts took care to be
out of the line of fire of the biggest
sneeze in the world.

So if ever you should be in Africa when the elephant-grass is in flower, and should chance to see a great tusker with the longest trunk you could possibly imagine – keep well away, and watch, and listen.

You will see that great tusker shut
his eyes and close his mouth and
stick his fantastically, unbelievably,
impossibly long trunk straight out
before him. And you will hear:

"AAAAAARCHOOOOOO!!!"

And then you know what to say,
don't you?

"BLESSU!"